Flip-Flops

Nancy Cote

Albert Whitman & Company
Morton Grove, Illinois

To my best friends,
Marie, Diane D., Charlotte,
JoAnne, Diane I., and Elaine. —N. C.

Library of Congress Cataloging-in-Publication Data
Cote, Nancy.
Flip-flops / written and illustrated by Nancy Cote.
p. cm.

Summary: Even though Penny is annoyed that she can
only find one of her flip-flops on the day she goes to the
beach, she discovers a number of uses for it and enjoys
her time there.
ISBN 0-8075-2504-9
[1. Beaches--Fiction. 2. Shoes--Fiction.] I. Title.
PZ7.C825Fl   1998
97-33143 [E]--dc21
CIP   AC

The paintings were done in gouache and colored pencil.
The text typeface is Friday Regular.
The design is by Scott Piehl.

Mama lifted the shade in Penny's bedroom window. The sun poured in.

"Can Penny come out to play?" called Charlotte.

"Not today," Mama answered. "Today is *our* beach day!"

Penny had forgotten that it was Mama's day off.
She'd forgotten about the beach. She jumped out of bed
and watched Charlotte join some girls playing double dutch.
What could she do? Mama was already packing the car.

After breakfast, Penny squeezed into last year's bathing suit and looked for her flip-flops. She could only find one.

"What *good* is this?" she complained.

Mama helped Penny search, but the missing flip-flop was nowhere to be found. So Penny hopped with one flop all the way to the car.

First they rode through the city, then over a bridge and past a dairy farm.

Penny knew they were close when they came to the stand that sold towels and beachballs, candy and pops, shovels and pails, and pairs of flip-flops. She crossed her fingers, hoping Mama would pull over.

"Look!" cried Mama. "I can see the ocean!"

And the car rolled on.

Soon they were at the beach.

Mama sat down to relax. Penny wished she could find someone to play with.

A woman sitting nearby was fanning herself. Penny didn't have a fan. All she had was a flip-flop. She took it off and waved it back and forth.

The woman winked at Penny.

"Do you have any children here today?" Penny asked her.

"I have two granddaughters just about your age, but they're away at camp," she said.

"I bet they're having fun," thought Penny.

By the water, she saw a girl building a sand castle.
Penny didn't have a shovel, but she did have a flip-flop.
She plopped down alongside the girl and began digging.
The girl smiled at Penny.

But suddenly, her big brother appeared and carried his giggling sister off for a swim.

At the shore, some boys were sailing toy boats. Penny didn't have a boat, but she did have a flip-flop. She joined the boys and won two out of three races!

Soon the boys were hungry. They gave Penny a high-five and raced home for lunch.

Penny sighed.

"Want to catch hermit crabs?" she heard someone ask. Penny turned around.

"My name is Meggie," said a girl. "Are you afraid
of crabs? I like them, but I'm afraid to pick them up."
"Me, too," agreed Penny, "but I have an idea."

She bent her flip-flop in half like a crab claw. Then she scooped up crabs and sand, and in no time she and Meggie had filled half a bucket without touching even one crab.

"You have great ideas!" Meggie said.

"I have a better idea," said Penny. "Let's be friends!"

Meggie did a back flip. Penny tried to flip but flopped onto the sand.

Meggie showed Penny how to roll, tumble, and spin across the beach.

That afternoon, with Penny's flip-flop, they played catch,

chased sea gulls,

rescued stranded starfish from the hot sun...

EVER

and wrote a special message in the sand. Together,
they made a perfect pair.

When it was time to go, Penny wrote Meggie's
phone number on the flip-flop and promised to call.

On their way home, Penny and Mama came to the stand that sold towels and beachballs, candy and pops, shovels and pails, and pairs of flip-flops.

Mama pulled the car over. "Would you like to get something here, Penny?" she asked.

Looking at her flip-flop, Penny smiled. "No thanks, Mama. I have everything I need."

"Me, too," Mama agreed.

And off they went, happy as clams.